This book belongs to

. . . .

Retold by Ronne Randall
Illustrated by Anna C. Leplar

This is a Parragon Publishing Book
First published in 2006

Parragon Publishing
Queen Street House
4 Queen Street
Bath BA1 1HE, UK

Copyright © Parragon Books Ltd 2006

ISBN 1-40545-124-6
Printed in Indonesia

Hans Christian Andersen

The Ugly Duckling

p

One sunny summer day, a mother duck built her nest among the reeds near the moat of an old castle. There she laid her eggs, and there she sat, keeping them warm, day after day.

Finally, the eggs began to crack. Peep! Peep! Out popped each fuzzy little duckling's head, one after another.

Mother Duck nuzzled each of her babies.

"Welcome," she quacked.

Then she noticed that one last egg, the biggest one of all, had not yet hatched.

"Oh, dear!" she said, sitting down again. "I wonder how much longer this one will take!"

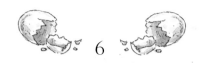

Finally, a long time later, the biggest egg began to crack.

"Honk! Honk!" said the duckling, tumbling out. He was much bigger and scruffier than the other ducklings.

"He's not as pretty as my other babies," Mother Duck said to herself. "But I'll look after him, just the same."

The next morning, Mother Duck took all her babies, even the big, ugly one, to the moat for their first swimming lesson.

They all followed her into the water, splish-splosh-splash, one by one. They all swam beautifully—and the big, ugly duckling swam best of all!

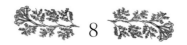

The other ducks came to watch.

"Who's that scruffy creature?" squawked one.

"He's my youngest duckling," said Mother Duck. "See how well he swims!"

"But he's so big, and so UGLY!" quacked the other ducks, laughing. While his brothers and sisters swam along, the little ugly duckling paddled into the reeds and tried to hide.

Mother Duck came over to him.

"Don't worry about those silly ducks," she told him. "I'll take you to the barnyard this afternoon. I'm sure the animals there will be kinder."

But she was wrong. As soon as the barnyard animals saw the ugly duckling, they began to laugh and shout.

"Most of your ducklings are lovely," clucked the hen. "But look at that big, scruffy, UGLY one! He's nothing like the others!"

"He's too ugly for this barnyard!" cackled the goose.

The pig snorted and said, "Why, he's the ugliest duckling I've ever seen!"

The little ugly duckling ran away and hung his head in shame.

The same thing happened the next day, and the day after that. The ducks on the moat and the animals in the barnyard all teased the ugly duckling, and chased him and called him names. Even his own brothers and sisters made fun of him and tried to peck him when they went swimming. The ugly duckling had no friends at all.

The ugly duckling was so sad and lonely that he decided to run away, out into the big, wide world. Early one morning, before anyone else was awake, he ran away, through the reeds, past the moat and the barnyard and the castle walls, till he came to a marsh.

There he saw a flock of wild ducks dabbling in the water.

"What kind of bird are you?" they asked.

"I'm a duckling," the ugly duckling replied.

"No, you're not," said the biggest duck. "You're much too ugly! We don't want to have anything to do with you!" And they turned away, leaving him alone.

The ugly duckling spent two lonely days on the marsh, far from the other ducks. Then, on the third day, a group of hunters came, scaring all the ducks away.

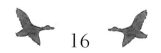

The frightened ugly duckling ran across the marsh and over fields and meadows. When he saw a cottage at the edge of the woods, he flew down and crawled in through a window, curled up in a corner of the kitchen and fell fast asleep.

An old woman lived in the cottage with her cat and her hen. The next morning, the cat and the hen found the ugly duckling.

"Can you lay eggs?" clucked the hen.

"No," said the ugly duckling.

"Can you catch mice?" meowed the cat.

"No," said the ugly duckling.

"Then you're useless!" said the cat.

"And you're VERY ugly!" added the hen.

"You'd better get out of here, before I scratch you!" hissed the cat.

19

So, once again, the ugly duckling ran away, out into the big, wide world.

The ugly duckling wandered far and wide until he came to a lake where he could swim and find food. There were other ducks there, but when they saw how ugly he was, they kept far away from him.

The ugly duckling stayed on the lake all summer. Then the fall came, and the weather began to grow cold. All the other ducks began to fly south, where the weather was warmer. The ugly duckling shivered by himself in the tall grass beside the lake.

One evening, just before sunset, the ugly duckling looked up and saw a flock of big, beautiful birds above him. Their white feathers gleamed in the rosy-gold sunlight, and they had long, graceful necks. They were flying south, just like the ducks.

The ugly duckling flapped his stubby wings and stretched his neck to watch them for as long as he could. They were so beautiful that he felt like crying.

"I wish I could go with them," he thought. "But they would never even look at someone as ugly as I am."

Fall turned to winter, and the lake froze solid. The ugly duckling couldn't swim any longer. His feathers were caked with ice and snow, and he couldn't find any food.

Luckily, a farmer found the ugly duckling and brought him home to his family. The farmer's wife warmed the ugly duckling up by the stove, and the farmer's children tried to play with him. But they were loud and rough, and the ugly duckling was frightened. He flapped his wings and knocked over a milk pail.

The children screamed and laughed, and tried to catch the ugly duckling, which only frightened him more. The ugly duckling flew across the kitchen—right into the flour bin! The farmer's wife chased him out of the house and into the yard, where he hid among some bushes.

Somehow, the ugly duckling found his way to a swamp, and there he managed to live for the rest of the long, hard winter.

At last spring came, bringing bright, warm sunshine. The ugly duckling spread his wings, and was amazed to find that they were big and strong. He flew up into the air and across the fields to a canal. There, swimming along the glassy water, he saw the beautiful birds he had seen last autumn.

"I'd better hide," he thought. "If they see me, they will just chase me and call me names like all the others have."

But when the birds saw him, they swam over to meet him.

"Hello!" they said.

 26

The ugly duckling looked around. He couldn't believe they were talking to him!

"We are swans," explained one of the birds. "And so are you—you are a very fine young swan indeed!"

The ugly duckling looked down at his reflection in the water. It was true—a handsome swan looked back at him!

The other swans made a circle around him and nuzzled him with their beaks. "Welcome," they said. "We would be happy to have you in our flock!"

The new young swan thought his heart would burst.

"I never dreamed I could be so happy," he thought, "when I was a little ugly duckling."

And, looking around at his new friends, he knew that he would be happy forever.

The End